WORD FAMILY
MiNi-STORYBOOKS

by Laura Johnsrud

SCHOLASTIC
PROFESSIONAL BOOKS

New York ✱ Toronto ✱ London ✱ Auckland ✱ Sydney
Mexico City ✱ New Delhi ✱ Hong Kong ✱ Buenos Aires

This book is dedicated to my own very special children, Darcy, Raymond, and Sara, and all of those children who have not yet discovered the magic of reading. A special thanks goes out to my "unofficial" publicist, Michaela, and my loving, supportive husband, Norm. Of course none of this would have happened without my terrific colleagues and friends at Sevastopol School—THANKS!

Cover design by Jim Sarfati
Interior design by Mindy Belter
Cover illustrations by Jane Dippold and Anne Kennedy
Interior illustrations by Jane Dippold (pages 17–24, 33–36, 61–68);
Anne Kennedy (pages 25–32, 41–48, 53–56); and
Tammie Lyon (pages 13–16, 37–40, 49–52, 57–60, 69–72)

ISBN: 0-439-22248-6

* CONTENTS *

Dear Colleague:

As educators, we are faced with the challenge of helping our students develop into lifelong learners. The debate continues, however, about which method or philosophy works best to help children reach this goal. Just as we wouldn't ask a carpenter to build a house with only a hammer, we cannot "equip" children with only one method. Like the carpenter, a young reader needs a variety of tools.

Phonological awareness is an important tool in the reader's toolbox. One way to build phonological awareness is to develop children's knowledge of word patterns through the study of word families. *Word Family Mini-Storybooks* provides a delightful and lively way to help children learn word families. Each of these 15 mini-books tells a lively, laugh-aloud story that reinforces two key word families. To nurture young readers, the mini-books feature rhyming, predictable text, illustrations that support the story, and a memorable cast of characters. They are designed to give children reading experiences that are positive and rewarding. When children feel success in reading, they are motivated to read even more.

As a reading specialist for the past 20 years, I have tried a myriad of reading programs, methods, and materials. From all of these experiences, I have come to believe strongly that we must always bring children back to a story. Skills taught in isolation are meaningless; they must be connected to text so that children can put their newly acquired skills into practice. *Word Family Mini-Storybooks* provides an easy way to teach skills in the context of enjoyable, age-appropriate stories. The mini-books also provide opportunities for children to think about, interpret, and ask questions about what they read.

The 30 word families in this program can be found in hundreds of primary grade words. Knowledge of these word families greatly enhances children's ability to decode words and boosts their skills in reading, writing, and spelling. And the more confident children are in their language skills, the more their enthusiasm for reading grows. A recent experience I had with my daughter convinced me of this reality. I was sitting upstairs on my comfy couch, after putting my two younger children to bed. It was my special writing time. As I began writing, my daughter Sara asked me, "What are you doing, Mom?"

"Writing."

"What are you writing?"

"Stuff." (Not one of my better parental moments.)

"Can I help?" Now, my first instinct was to say no, but something inspired me.

"Sure! I need help making lists of words for my word family books. I'll give you the word family, the letters of the alphabet, and some blends. Try to make as many words as you can for each word family, using the letters and the blends." I did a few examples and then she took off. For an hour she made word lists and generated over 90 words! Not only did the experience provide some quality time for the two of us but it also allowed my daughter to have fun with words—something that had always been difficult for her.

I hope that these mini-books help you give each of your students a valuable addition to their reader's toolbox. I also hope you and your students enjoy reading these word family stories as much as I enjoyed writing them.

Laura Johnsrud

✱ HOW TO USE THIS BOOK ✱

The mini-storybooks can be used in a variety of ways and can be easily integrated into your current reading program. Use the mini-books as:

- *mini-lessons introducing the featured word families.*
- *shared reading experiences.*
- *extensions of spelling lessons.*
- *springboards for creative writing assignments.*
- *whole-group lessons prior to guided reading.*
- *independent activities at a reading center.*
- *take-home reading assignments.*

Each mini-book features words from two word families, providing lots of opportunities for children to look for word patterns. The word families in each book begin with the same vowel, so children have the additional challenge of distinguishing between them. The reproducible mini-book format is a great learning tool because it allows children to highlight words, using a different color for each word family. Show children how to assemble the books (see directions on page 6), and then invite them to color the illustrations.

The next few pages outline a general lesson plan. The Story Notes section on pages 7–10 provides additional information about each story, including vocabulary words and discussion questions. You'll also find a reproducible Graphic Organizer on page 11 and a Reading Log on page 12. I encourage you to adapt and add to these ideas as you see fit, to best meet your students' needs and interests. Keep in mind that the purpose of this book is to teach word patterns in an engaging way—so don't hesitate to get silly and have fun with the stories!

INTRODUCING THE STORY

- Begin the lesson with a thought-provoking question that will get children thinking about the story and activate their memories of their own experiences. It is helpful for children to draw on personal experiences to make sense of a story.
- Discuss the title of the book and ask children to make predictions about the story. Look at the illustration on the cover and ask children to point out details that might provide clues about what will happen.
- If children need extra support, take a "picture walk" through the book. (Avoid showing the last few pages so that you don't give away the ending.)
- Discuss vocabulary words and concepts that may be unfamiliar to children. (Vocabulary words are listed in the Story Notes on pages 7–10.)
- Introduce the featured word families. Read aloud the title, and ask children to guess which word families will be in the book. Write the two word families on the chalkboard and brainstorm a list of words from each word family. Explain that you will read a story that includes many of these words, and encourage children to listen closely to see how many of them they hear.

READING THE STORY

- **For emergent readers:** Read the story aloud, inviting children to join in as you read the repetitive parts.
- **For fluent readers:** Challenge children to read the books on their own. Assist with new vocabulary words, as necessary.
- Pause at various points in the story and ask children to predict what will happen on the next page.

REFLECTING

- Ask children a series of discussion questions, such as "What did you like about the story? Was the ending a surprise? What made it surprising?" Add any other questions that encourage them to reflect upon the story. (See Story Notes for additional discussion questions.)
- Reread the story, pausing several times to discuss new concepts or vocabulary words. (See Story Notes for ideas.)

STUDYING THE WORD FAMILIES

- Challenge children to reread the story and look for words that belong in the featured word families. You might have them highlight the words in a different color for each word family.
- Give each child a copy of the reproducible Graphic Organizer on page 11. Have children list the words they find and then add any additional words. Once students have read all of the mini-storybooks, they will have 30 word family lists. Bind these pages together with a cover and a few additional pages so that each child has his or her own word family reference book. Children can refer to these lists for help with writing, reading, and spelling.
- Create a classroom word wall in a highly visible place. Each time you introduce a mini-book, add words from the two word families to the word wall.

WRITING

- Have children create additional pages for the mini-book.
- Invite children to write a new ending.
- Challenge children to create their own story using the words from the two word families featured in the book. Encourage children to refer to the words they listed on their Graphic Organizer.
- Invite students to share their new pages, endings, and stories with a partner, a small group, or the whole class.

USING THE READING LOG

- The Reading Log provides an easy way to keep track of the stories children have read. (This is especially useful if children read the books on their own.) After a student has read a story and filled in the Graphic Organizer, it is a good idea to set up a brief meeting. Have the student read parts of the story for you to assess his or her fluency and familiarity with the featured word families. Then ask the student to find words from the word families. Check the appropriate boxes on the Reading Log when a student has successfully completed all steps.

HOW TO ASSEMBLE THE BOOKS

1. Carefully remove the mini-book to be copied, tearing along the perforation.

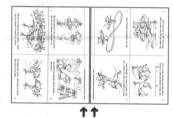

2. Make double-sided copies of the mini-book pages. *Note: If your copy machine does not have a double-sided function, first make copies of the title page. Place these copies in the paper tray with the blank side facing up. Next, make a copy of the mini-book pages so that page 3 copies directly behind page 2. Make a test copy to be sure the pages are positioned correctly. Repeat these steps with the remaining pages so that page 7 copies directly behind page 6.*

3. Cut each page in half along the solid line.

4. Place the pages in numerical order. Fold along the dotted line.

   Pages 9 & 6 →
   Pages 11 & 4 →
   Pages 13 & 2 →
   Pages 15 & cover →

5. Staple the pages together along the book's spine.

Listed on the following pages are a few teaching ideas for each of the mini-books. I would love to hear about any additional activities that you develop for these stories. Please send or e-mail your ideas to me: Laura Johnsrud, 6337 County OO, Sturgeon Bay, WI 54235, or Ljohnsru@doorpi.net.

A BIRTHDAY BASH HAT
Word Families: -ash, -at,
Vocabulary: bash, sash, splash, clash, dash, slash, drooped

Choose a word family that is not featured in this story and brainstorm a list of words that belong in that word family. Then invite children to make up their own stories in which Mrs. Pat adds even more items to her hat. Have children incorporate words from the class-generated list. Invite them to illustrate their stories with humorous pictures.

GRANDPA DAN'S NAP
Word Families: -an, -ap
Vocabulary: curled

Lead a discussion about naps. Ask: "Do you ever like taking a nap? What kind of environment is good for napping? How do you feel when someone wakes you up? Why do grownups seem to enjoy naps more than children do?" Read the story aloud. Then read it again as a choral reading, with students adding sound effects for "Rap! Rap! Rap!" and "Tap! Tap! Tap!" For a writing exercise, introduce a new word family and brainstorm a list of words in that word family. Invite students to add pages to the story, showing Grandpa Dan's other friends returning various objects to him. Encourage children to use words from the class-generated list.

RAY'S FAMOUS CAKE
Word Families: -ay, -ake
Vocabulary: delay, batter, quake, sway

Discuss cooking experiences children have had. Ask: "What did you cook? What ingredients did you use? How long did it take to prepare the food? What do you like or dislike about cooking?" As you read the story aloud, invite children to perform movement that reflects the action on each page. This book provides a good springboard for talking about verbs.

Word Families: *-eep, -et*

THE SHEEP GET IN THEIR JEEP
Word Families: *-eep, -et*
Vocabulary: steep, hairnet, fret, boarding
Talk about the different means of transportation children have used. Ask whether they have ever been on a trip that seemed to take a very long time. What do children do to pass the time? Teach a mini-lesson on quotation marks, and then have children find the quotation marks on pages 1–14 of the mini-book. You might have children highlight the sentence that is spoken on each of these pages. When reading the story aloud, have a volunteer read all of Little Sheep's lines.

Word Families: *-ell, -est*

NELL AND PEST
Word Families: *-ell, -est*
Vocabulary: spell, dwell, swampy, jest, zest, pest
After reading the story aloud, ask children to think about the characters in the story. If they were Pest, would they trust Nell? Why or why not? What information in the story helped them reach this conclusion? Have children read the story in pairs, with one child reading the part of Nell and the other reading the part of Pest.

Encourage children to be dramatic, and then invite volunteers to read aloud for the class.

Word Families: *-ill, -ack*

JILL LEARNS TO PACK
Word Families: *-ill, -ack*
Vocabulary: chill, frill
Ask children about their experiences sleeping over at friends' or relatives' homes. Was it difficult deciding what to pack? Ask why Jill had such a difficult time packing. What advice would they give Jill about packing? Have children make a list of all the objects Jill packed and then cross off things she could have left at home. Ask: "Is there anything she forgot that she might need?"

Word Families: *-in, -ick*

MRS. FLIN GETS SICK
Word Families: *-in, -ick*
Vocabulary: flick, tin, sharp, prick, click, loss
Divide the class into small groups and have each group act out the story. You might have one child in each group be the director. Explain that the director's job is to help the actors decide what movements to do and what kind of emotion to add to the skit.

Word Families: *-ing, -ink*

THE KING'S PINK LEMONADE
Word Families: *-ing, -ink*
Vocabulary: roared, stared, sting

Ask children to imagine what it would be like to be a king or queen. What would they like or dislike about it? When reading the story, have children act out the king's actions. Invite children to read the part of the king. How many different-sounding roars can they make? After reading the story, ask children what lesson the king learned.

Word Families: *-it, -ip*

MR. WIT'S CAMPING TRIP
Word Families: *-it, -ip*
Vocabulary: lickety split, snagged

Lead a discussion about camping or outdoor experiences children have had. If children have never been camping, ask them to imagine what it might be like. What would they like or dislike about camping? Would they miss any conveniences they have at home? Ask why Mr. Wit had so much trouble on his trip. Would children have done anything differently to prevent such problems?

Word Families: *-ine, -ight*

THREE SWINE DINE ONE NIGHT
Word Families: *-ine, -ight*
Vocabulary: swine, dine, might, pine, tuxedos, twine, curled, divine, delight

Ask children what they would do to get ready for an important evening. When reading the story aloud, encourage children to act out the actions in the story. After reading, invite children to draw pictures of the pigs before, during, and after dinner. What do children think the pigs ate for dinner?

Word Families: *-ice, -ide*

TWO MICE GLIDE ON ICE
Word Families: *-ice, -ide*
Vocabulary: glide, advice, entice, worldwide, stride, collide

Have a class discussion about performances that children have attended (including school assemblies). What do they enjoy about being in the audience? Ask whether they have ever been in a performance. What do they enjoy about performing? After reading the story, invite children to draw posters advertising the Mice on Ice show. Encourage them to add a description of the show, including words from the *-ice* and *-ide* word families.

MR. BLOCK'S BIG SNORE
Word Families: *-ock, -ore*
Vocabulary: bore, gentle, shock, sore, chore, flock, adore

Ask children whether they have ever heard anyone snoring. What is the funniest sounding snore they can imagine? After reading the story, ask children what problems Mr. Block's snoring caused for other characters in the story. Can children think of other solutions to the problem besides the one in the book?

MRS. POP'S AWFUL SPOT
Word Families: *-op, -ot*
Vocabulary: gooey, glop

Talk about ways to get a carpet clean. Ask children what they have seen their family members do at home to clean the carpet. Do their methods always work? Ask children what they thought of Mrs. Pop's solution at the end of the story. Would they have done anything differently to try to get the spot out?

MR. CRUMP COLLECTS JUNK
Word Families: *-ump, -unk*
Vocabulary: dump, marvelous, rusty, pogo stick, birdbath, dunk, stump, gunk, ragged

Discuss the expression "One man's trash is another man's treasure." Have children ever found anything at a yard sale that they treasure? Before reading, review the months of the year and introduce adjectives. After reading, challenge children to find the adjectives in the story. Then invite children to write their own stories about finding junk, and encourage them to use interesting adjectives to describe the objects.

MRS. CLUG'S DUCK
Word Families: *-ug, -uck*
Vocabulary: longed, cozy, snug, pluck, shiny, bill

Lead a discussion about pets. What kinds of pets do students have? Have they ever heard of anyone having a pet duck? After reading the story, ask children what they would have done to get Chuck to quack. Introduce other word families and brainstorm lists of words in those word families. Invite children to write their own silly pet stories using words from the class-generated lists.

Name _____ **Date** _____

Book Title _____

Word Family Graphic Organizer

Look for the two word families that appear on the book's cover. At the top of each column, write one word family. Then look in the book for words that belong in that word family. Write the words on the lines. If you can think of more words, add them to your lists.

Word Family _____   **Word Family** _____

_____   _____

_____   _____

_____   _____

_____   _____

_____   _____

_____   _____

_____   _____

_____   _____

_____   _____

_____   _____

_____   _____

Name _____ Date _____

Reading Log

	Student has read the mini-book.	Student has filled out the Graphic Organizer.	Student recognizes words in Word Family 1.	Student recognizes words in Word Family 2.
A Birthday Bash Hat *-ash, -at*				
Grandpa Dan's Nap *-an, -ap*				
Ray's Famous Cake *-ay, -ake*				
The Sheep Get in Their Jeep *-eep, -et*				
Nell and Pest *-ell, -est*				
Jill Learns to Pack *-ill, -ack*				
Mrs. Flin Gets Sick *-in, -ick*				
The King's Pink Lemonade *-ing, -ink*				
Three Swine Dine One Night *-ine, -ight*				
Mr. Wit's Camping Trip *-it, -ip*				
Two Mice Glide on Ice *-ice, -ide*				
Mr. Block's Big Snore *-ock, -ore*				
Mrs. Pop's Awful Spot *-op, -ot*				
Mr. Crump Collects Junk *-ump, -unk*				
Mrs. Clug's Duck *-ug, -uck*				

Word Family Mini-Storybooks Scholastic Professional Books

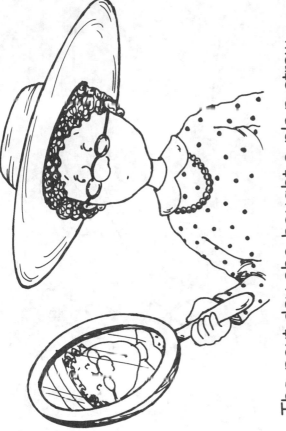

The next day she bought a plain straw hat. "This hat's too flat," said Mrs. Pat.

A Birthday Bash Hat

Word Families: -ash, -at

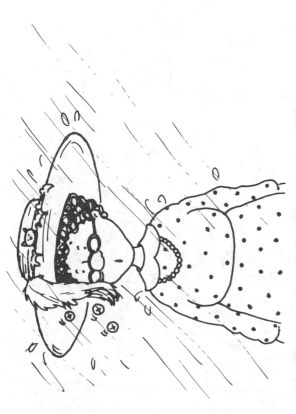

The buttons fell into a puddle with a big splash.

Mrs. Pat's new hat was now quite flat. "Oh, drat! No hat for the birthday bash!" said Mrs. Pat.

First, she added a sash to the hat.

"That is better," said Mrs. Pat.

The feathers drooped and gave her a rash.

Mrs. Pat was invited to a birthday bash.

"I need a new hat," said Mrs. Pat.

The cat pin fell to the ground with a loud crash.

Then she added a pin shaped like a cat. "Some dash for my hat," said Mrs. Pat.

6

Then she added bright pink flowers to the hat. "A splash of color!" said Mrs. Pat.

4

Mrs. Pat put on her new hat. Then she stepped outside onto the mat.

9

The bright pink flowers started to look like mash.

11

7

Next, she added gold buttons to the hat. "These are from my favorite stash," said Mrs. Pat.

5

Next, she added blue feathers to the hat. "I hope they don't clash," said Mrs. Pat.

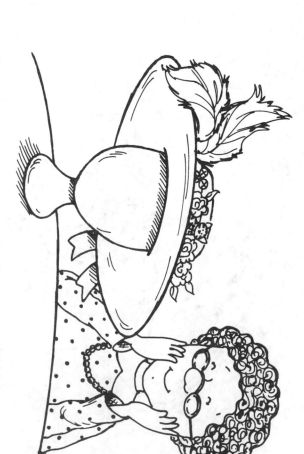

8

She was finally ready for the birthday bash. "Oh, my! Some hat!" said Mrs. Pat.

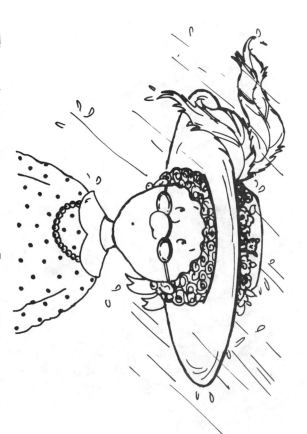

10

The sky became gray. It started to rain. Raindrops fell on her hat with a splat!

Rap! Rap! Rap!
Tap! Tap! Tap!

2

Grandpa Dan's Nap

Word Families: -an, -ap

Grandpa Dan sat down. The cat curled up in his lap. It was time for an afternoon nap! *Zzzzzzzzzzzz!*

13

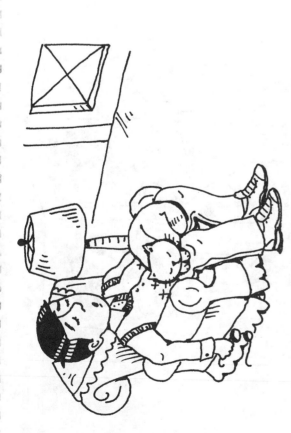

"Today is not a good day for an afternoon nap!"

15

Grandpa Dan said, "How can I nap
with a sound like that?"

Grandpa Dan ran to the door. It was
his friend Fran. Fran was returning
Grandpa Dan's pan.

Grandpa Dan took off his cap. The
cat curled up on Grandpa Dan's lap.
It was time for an afternoon nap.

"Yap! Yap! Yap!"

Rap! Rap! Rap!
Tap! Tap! Tap!

Grandpa Dan ran to the docr. It was his friend Stan. Stan was returning Grandpa Dan's fan.

Grandpa Dan sat down. The cat curled up in his lap. It was time for an afternoon nap.

Grandpa Dan said, "How can I nap with a sound like that?"

Grandpa Dan said, "How can I nap
with a sound like that?"

Grandpa Dan ran to the door. It was
his friend Pap. Pap was returning
Grandpa Dan's map.

Grandpa Dan sat down. The cat
curled up in his lap. It was time for
an afternoon nap.

Rap! Rap! Rap!
Tap! Tap! Tap!

One day Ray decided to make his famous coconut cake.

2

Ray's Famous Cake

Word Families: *-ay, -ake*

His legs began to quake. The tray started to shake.

13

Hooray! Ray saved the day! Now he can give the cake to Jake, Drake, and Kay.

15

He took out his gray spoon and his big bowl made of clay.

But then his foot got stuck on a rake!

12

Ray loved to bake. He would rather bake than play.

The cake began to sway. Then the cake fell, but Ray caught it with the rake!

14

He mixed butter, sugar, vanilla, and eggs. There was no time to delay!

Next, he added baking powcer and flour with a shake.

When the cake had cooled, Ray frosted it with speed. Tasting was only a minute away!

Ray lifted the tray and was on his way.

He beat the egg whites just the right way. Then he mixed them into the batter for half a day.

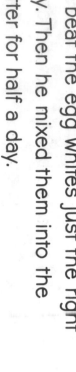

Then he added the coconut, flake by flake.

Ray put the cake in the oven. It would take 30 minutes to bake.

At last the cake was ready. Ray set it on a tray. He was going to bring it to his friends Jake, Drake, and Kay.

They drove past their friend and gave the horn a beep. "Are we there yet?" asked Little Sheep.

2

The Sheep Get in Their Jeep

Word Families: -eep, -et

They drove past some cows boarding a jet. Little Sheep asked, "Are we there yet?"

13

When they arrived, Little Sheep did not make a peep. In the back of the jeep, she was fast asleep.

15

They drove past some fish in a pool that was deep. "Are we there yet?" asked Little Sheep.

They drove past a boy with a huge, funny pet. Little Sheep asked, "Are we there yet?"

"Let us get ready to leave," said Papa Sheep. When they were ready, they got in their jeep.

They drove past the sun, which was starting to set. Little Sheep asked, "Are we there yet?"

They drove past some chicks that were learning to cheep. "Are we there yet?" asked Little Sheep.

6

They drove past some ducks that liked to mop and sweep. "Are we there yet?" asked Little Sheep.

4

They drove past a cat that was wearing a hairnet. Little Sheep asked, "Are we there yet?"

9

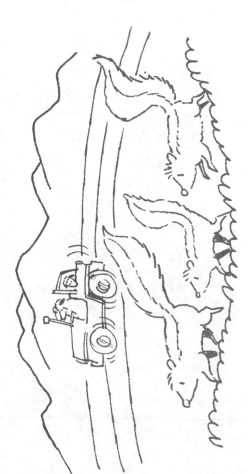

They drove past some skunks on their way to the vet. Little Sheep asked, "Are we there yet?"

11

They drove past some frogs that they once had met. Little Sheep asked, "Are we there yet?"

7

They drove past some rabbits on a slide that was steep. "Are we there yet?" asked Little Sheep.

5

They drove past some seals that were happy and wet. Little Sheep asked, "Are we there yet?"

8

They drove past a monkey that was starting to fret. Little Sheep asked, "Are we there yet?"

10

"How are you today?" asked the frog.

"My name is Nell."

2

Nell and Pest

Word Families: *-ell*, *-est*

"I don't agree," said Pest. "I prefer a

smell with more zest."

13

"Please leave me alone," said the fly.

"You're being a pest!"

15

"My name is Pest," said the fly.
"I am feeling quite well."

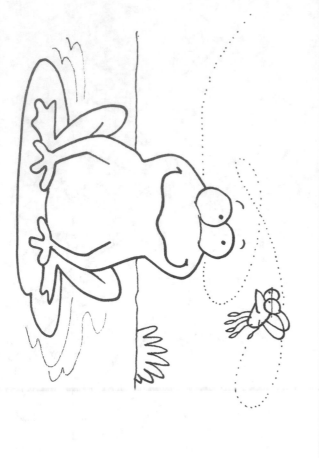

"Surely you jest! The smell is the best."

Nell was a frog. Pest was a fly. They met one day as Pest flew right by.

"Why don't you try it?" asked Nell.
"Just give it a test."

"But you must be tired from flying.
A rest would be best."

"You look sleepy," said Nell.
"Come here and sit a spell."

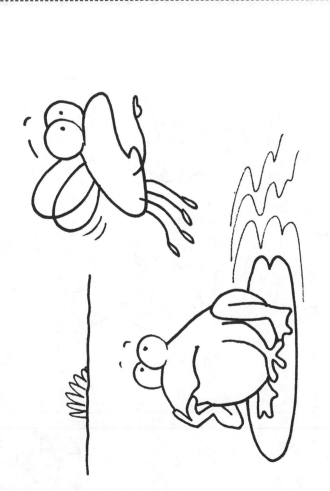

"But I must be going. I have to fly west."

"No, thank you," said Pest. "It has
a swampy smell."

"No. You would eat me. I can tell!" said Pest.

"No, thank you," said Pest. "I don't need a rest."

"Don't be silly," said Nell. "I just want a guest."

"Come see my home," said Nell. "Come see where I dwell."

Jill's mother gave Jill a bag to fill.
"Don't forget to pack your pajamas, Jill."

Jill Learns to Pack

Word Families: *-ill, -ack*

. . . and then her favorite plant from
the windowsill.

"Can Sue and Jack come here
instead?" asked Jill. "If I ask them
nicely, I think they will."

"First, I'll pack my teddy bear, Bill. And I'll pack a scarf in case of a chill."

Next, Jill put in her pet fish, named Gill . . . .

Jill was going to visit her cousins, Sue and Jack. "This will be fun! I need to pack!"

"Okay, Mom! There's nothing left to pack," said Jill.

Then she took down her red hat from the rack. Next, she added her toy zebra, Zack.

"Should I pack my mittens? I think I will. I'm packing so well. I pack with such skill!"

Next, she saw her toy train and track. Jill said to herself, "I'll bring those for Jack."

Maybe she should take her glass frog, named Lack, and some glue in case he should crack.

Jill put her socks in a stack. "Which shoes will be better? The blue or the black?"

"But what if I'm hungry? I'll need a snack." Jill packed a snack in a brown paper sack.

She was almost done when she saw her duck, Mack. In he went with a quack, quack, quack, quack!

She packed a towel in case she should spill. It was her fancy towel, the one with the frill.

Mrs. Flin Gets Sick

Word Families: -in, -ick

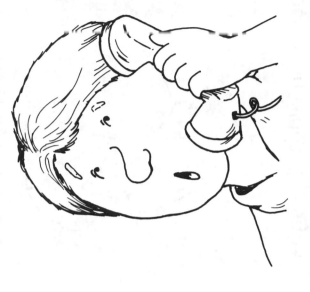

"I'l pick up the phone," said Nick. "I'll call Doctor Fin." Luckily, the doctor was in.

2

"Now, Mrs. Flin, I'm going to tap your knee. Oh, my, that's quite a kick!"

13

"Mrs. Flin, the spot is gone. No big loss. Your spot was only tomato sauce!"

15

The doctor arrived. "What's the problem?" he asked. "Let's see if we can fix it quick."

"Oh, ick! I'm very sick! Maybe you should call my twin brother, Rick."

"Call the doctor! I feel sick!" said Mrs. Flin to her husband, Nick.

"I'm very sick," said Mrs. Flin. "Is the big red spot still on my chin?"

"Oh, ick! I'm very sick. My head feels
as heavy as a brick!"

"I'm very sick," said Mrs. Fin.
"I have a big red spot on my chin."

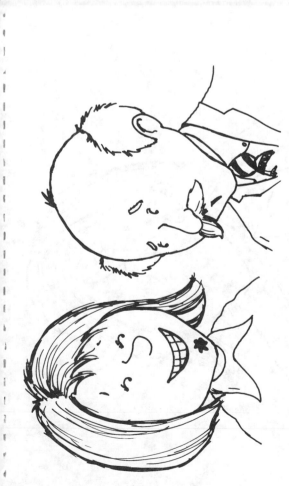

"Now, Mrs. Flin, open your mouth and
show me a grin. Just as I thought,
your teeth are all in."

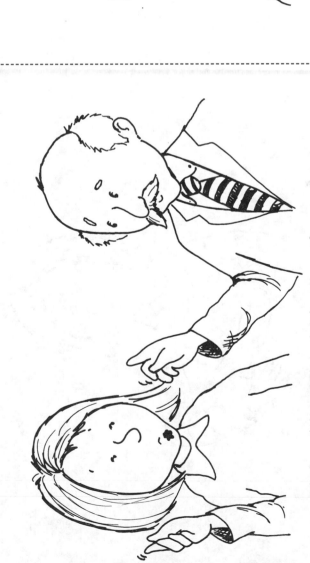

"Now, Mrs. Flin, let's see if you can
make your fingers click."

"Now, Mrs. Flin, let's see if you can walk and spin."

"I'm very sick," said Mrs. Flin.
"My head feels like it's made of tin."

"Now, Mrs. Flin, let's check your ears. I'll flick on my light and take a look within."

"Oh, ick! I'm very sick! I feel a sharp pain, like a pinprick."

He rang his bell with a
ding-a-ling-ling.

The King's Pink Lemonade

Word Families: *-ing, -ink*

The note said the king had forgotten
one thing: Everyone needs manners,
even a king.

13

". . . please."

15

"Bring me pink lemonade!"
roared the king.

The king was thirsty. He wanted a
drink. "I'd like pink lemonade, I think."

Someone wrote a note in black ink.
The king read the note, and his
face turned quite pink.

This made the king think. He asked
for a drink. But this time he said . . .

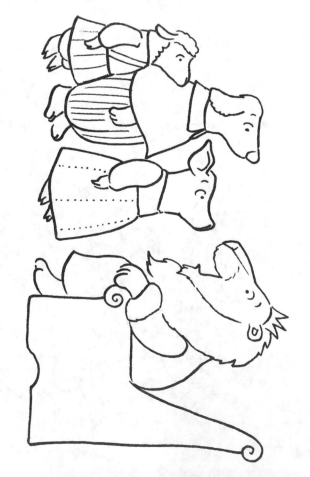

He stared and he stared. His eyes did not blink.

He shook his paw. He waved his big ring.

"Bring me pink lemonade!" roared the king.

He waited and waited. His heart started to sink. "Bring me pink lemonade. Where is my drink?"

"Bring me pink lemonade. Where is my drink?"

"Bring me pink lemonade!" roared the King.

He grew quite angry. His eyes started to sting.

He tapped his claws with a ping-a-ping-ping. "Bring me pink lemonade!" roared the King.

They scrubbed themselves with all their might. Those three fine swine were quite a sight!

2

Three Swine Dine One Night

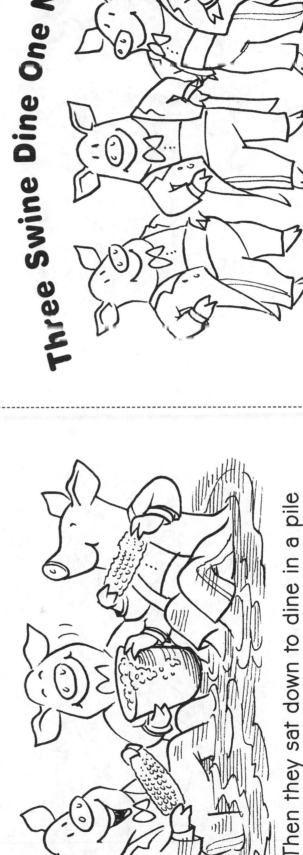

Word Families: -ine, -ight

They had good manners. They would never fight. Those three fine swine were quite a sight!

13

Then they sat down to dine in a pile of . . . MUD! What a delight! Those three muddy swine were quite a sight!

15

The swine now smelled like nice, fresh pine. What a sight, those three fine swine!

Three fine swine got ready to dine. They had plans to leave right at nine.

At last they were ready to go out for the night. Those three fine swine were quite a sight!

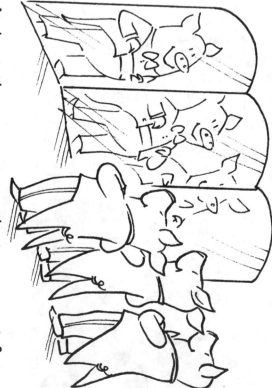

They walked down the road in a nice, neat line. What a sight, those three fine swine!

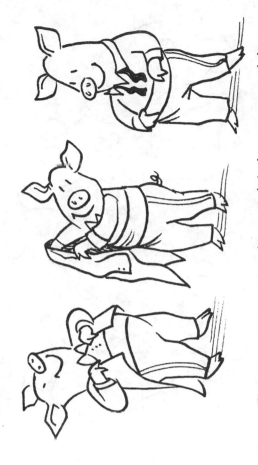

They wore tuxedos, which were a bit tight. Those three fine swine were quite a sight!

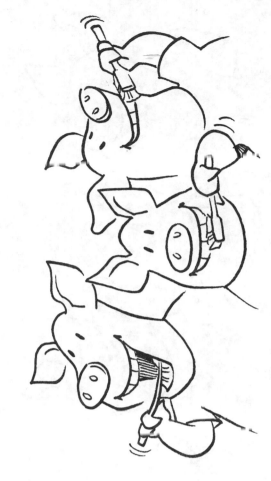

They brushed their teeth so they would shine. What a sight, those three fine swine!

Their eyes twinkled bright in the evening light. Those three fine swine were quite a sight!

Another said, "Thank you. It's almost nine." What a sight, those three fine swine!

They curled each of their tails like a little vine. What a sight, those three fine swine!

They pointed their ears to the left and right. Those three fine swine were quite a sight!

Then they flossed with some pieces of twine. What a sight, those three fine swine!

One said, "You look divine, dear friends of mine." What a sight, those three fine swine!

Mr. Wit's Camping Trip

Word Families: *-it, -ip*

He set up his tent, lickety split.

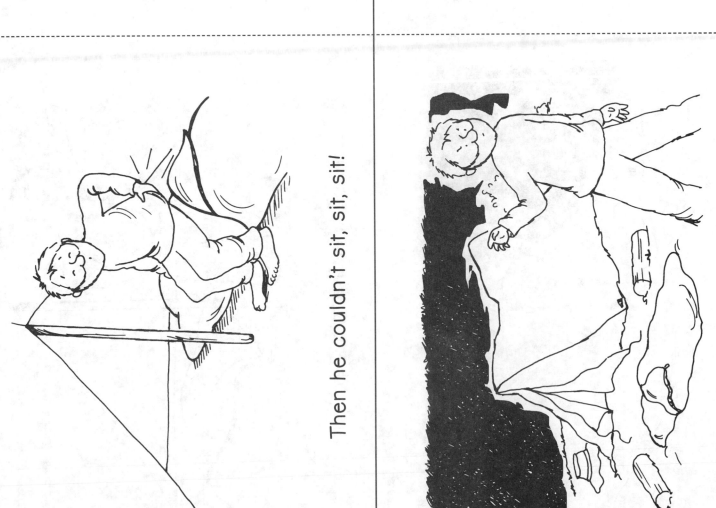

Then he couldn't sit, sit, sit!

"Oh, forget it!" said Mr. Wit. "I QUIT!"

3 He split some wood. Chip, chip, chip!

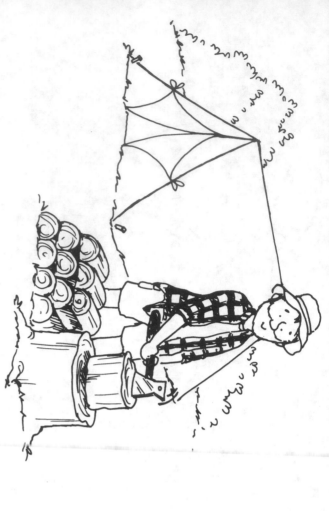

1 Mr. Wit was going camping. "Yippee! I'm going on a trip, trip, trip!"

He bumped his hip, hip, hip!

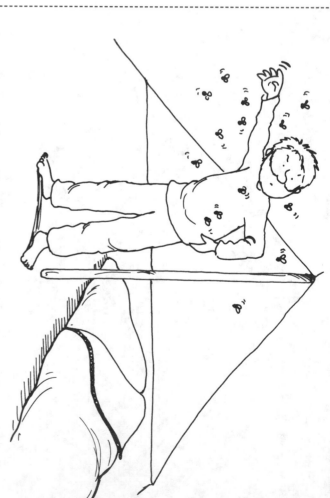

12

The animals outside went "Yip! Yip! Yip!"

14

It began to rain. Drip, drip, drip!

Then he snagged his pants. Rip, rip, rip!

His sleeping bag would not zip, zip, zip!

Bugs flew into the tent and bit, bit, bit!

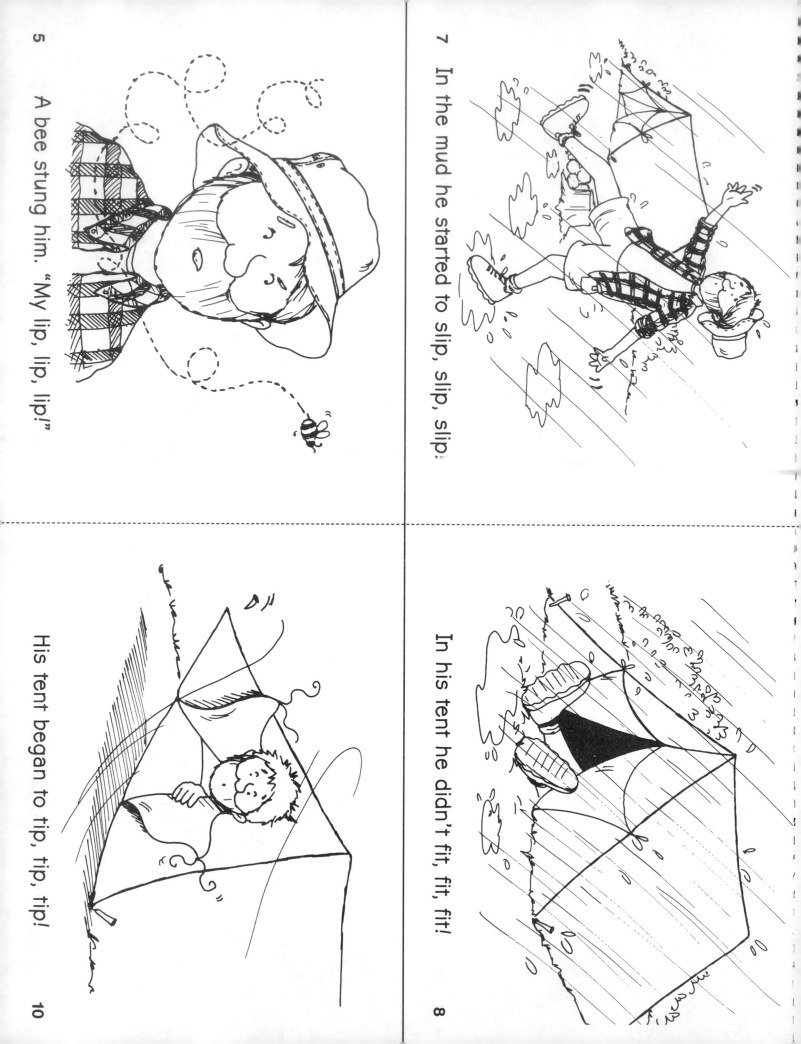

5 A bee stung him. "My lip, lip, lip, lip!"

7 In the mud he started to slip, slip, slip!

His tent began to tip, tip, tip! 10

In his tent he didn't fit, fit, fit! 8

Across the ice, we slide and glide.
We are famous far and wide!

2

Two Mice Glide on Ice

Word Families: *-ice, -ide*

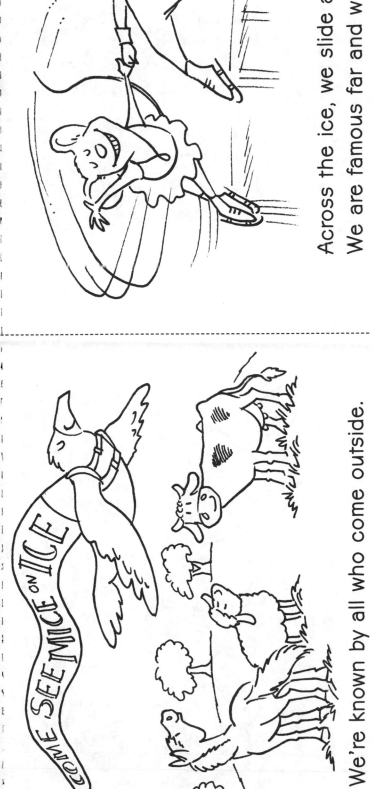

COME SEE MICE ON ICE

We're known by all who come outside.

13

. . . not to collide!

15

We spin around, not once but twice.
We are the famous mice on ice!

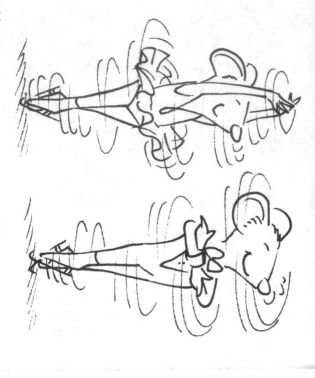

Our fame has spread. We're known
worldwide.

We are the famous mice on ice. Come
see our show! It's worth the price.

We skate with pride. We move in stride.
And we try our best . . .

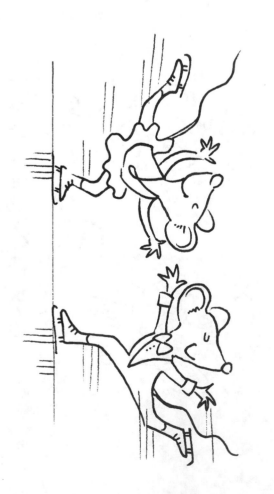

You can watch us slice the ice.
We are the famous skating mice!

We skate all day from side to side.
We'll even give a nice fun ride!

You'll be glad you took our advice. You
don't want to miss the skating mice!

Our fancy moves are sure to entice.
Come see the famous mice on ice!

Now it's time for you to decide.
Will you let us be your guide?

You can cheer. You can clap. You can
even throw rice! We are the famous
mice on ice!

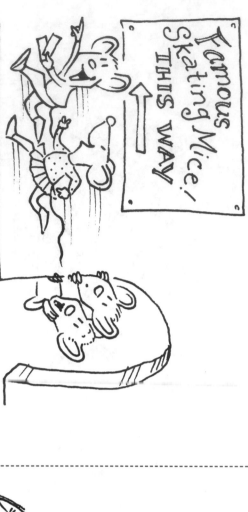

Come see our show! Don't stay inside!
You'll be glad you didn't hide.

Give your life some joy and spice!
Watch us skate and juggle dice.

He yawned and stretched and looked at the clock. I'll take a quick nap, thought Mr. Block.

Mr. Block's Big Snore

Word Families: -ock, -ore

"What do we do? We can't take any more. We can't take even one more big snore!"

. . .yelled, "WAKE UP!" Mr. Block's big snore was no more.

3   Soon Mr. Block began to snore.

1
a bore.

Mr. Block spent the day at the shore.
He was reading a book and found it

The people came together in a big
flock. How could they stop Mr. Block?

12

Then a small boy, whom we all adore,
made his way down the shore. He stopped
near Mr. Block's ear and then . . .

14

It was gentle at first, a soft, quiet snore.
But then it grew louder than it was before.

Then all of the chairs began to rock.
Everyone got up, except Mr. Block.

The waves began to crash against
the dock! Everyone worried, except
Mr. Block.

Somebody said, "Let's get a sock!"
But no one was brave enough to stop
Mr. Block.

His umbrella tore and blew down the shore. Everyone heard Mr. Block's big snore!

The sound of the snore was quite a shock. How could it come from Mr. Block?

Even walking became quite a chore. All because of Mr. Block's snore.

Everyone's ears were getting sore. They were all tired of listening to Mr. Block's big snore.

Mrs. Pop took a rag to blot the spot.

Blot! Blot! Blot!

2

Mrs. Pop's Awful Spot

Word Families: -op, -ot

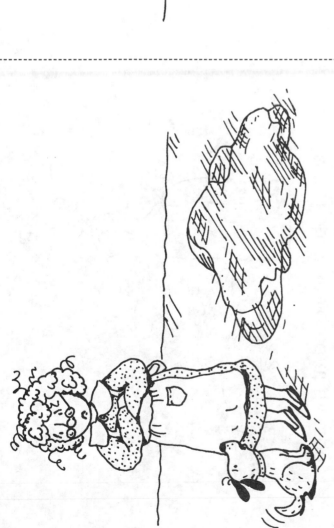

Did the spot go away? No, it did not!

13

. . . a rug!

15

Did the spot go away? No, it did not!

Mrs. Pop spilled some gooey glop.
Now the carpet had a tiny spot.

Mrs. Pop even yelled at the spot.
"Stop! Stop! Stop!"

Finally, Mrs. Pop said, "I'll fix that spot!"
And then she got . . .

Mrs. Pop put some cleaning glop on
top of the spot. Glop! Glop! Glop!

Mrs. Pop grabbed a mop and
mopped the spot. Flop! Flop! Flop!

Did the spot go away? No, it did not!

Did the spot go away? No, it did not!

Did the spot go away? No, it did not!

Mrs. Pop poured a pot of hot water on the spot. Slop! Slop! Slop!

Did the spot go away? No, it did not!

Mrs. Pop tried to hop on the spot. Hop! Hop! Hop!

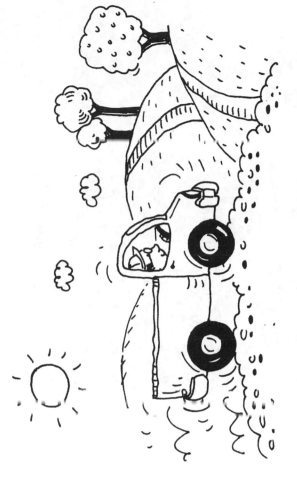

Once a month he drove his big truck to the dump. Clunk, clunk, clunk.

2

Mr. Crump Collects Junk

Word Families: -ump, -unk

In November he found a ragged teddy bear. Plump, plump, plump!

13

"Oh, no! A skunk, skunk, skunk, skunk!"

15

In January he found an old piano.
Plunk, plunk, plunk!

In October he found a pile of
dirty plates. Gunk, gunk, gunk!
Oh, marvelous junk!

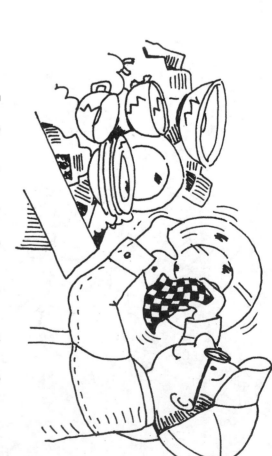

Mr. Crump loved to collect junk.

In December he found a big smelly
trunk. Inside he heard a sound.
Thunk, thunk, thunk!

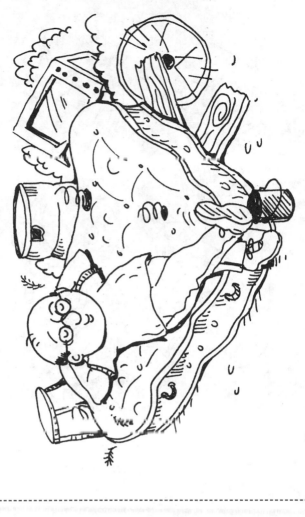

In April he found a feather mattress.
Lump, lump, lump! Oh, marvelous junk!

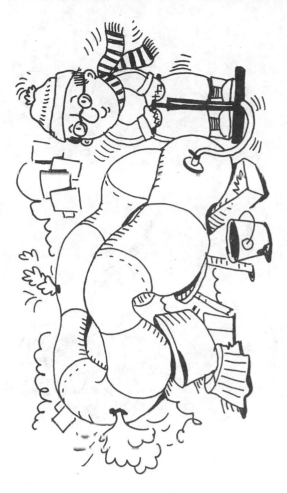

In February he found a rubber raft.
Pump, pump, pump! Oh, marvelous junk!

In July he found a big white bathtub.
Sunk, sunk, sunk!

In September he found a rocking
horse. Bump, bump, bump!

In May he found a purple pogo stick. Jump, jump, jump!

In March he found a rusty wagon. Thump, thump, thump!

In June he found a birdbath. Dunk, dunk, dunk! Oh, marvelous junk!

In August he found a pair of rusty roller skates. Stump, stump, stump!

But Chuck wouldn't quack.

Was his beak stuck?

Mrs. Clug's Duck

Word Families: -ug, -uck

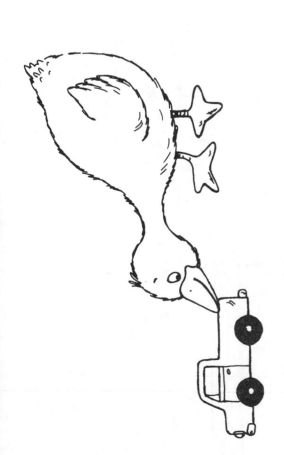

"I'll let him play with my shiny toy truck. Quack, Chuck, quack!" But she had no luck.

Moooooo . . . . .

Chuck lifted his head, stuck out his bill, and began to . . . . Moooooooooo!

"Aw, shucks!"

3

Mrs. Clug wanted to help her pet duck. She longed to hear a quack or even a cluck!

1

Mrs. Clug loved her pet duck, Chuck.

12

"I'll put him in a wagon and give him a tug. Quack, Chuck, quack!" But she had no luck.

14

Finally she said, "I know what you need, Chuck. You need a great big hug!"

"I'll give him tea in a mug. Quack, Chuck, quack!" But she had no luck.

"I'll wrap him in a blanket, nice and snug. Quack, Chuck, quack!" But she had no luck.

"I'll plug in some soft music. Quack, Chuck, quack!" But she had no luck.

"I'll give him water in a jug. Quack, Chuck, quack!" But she had no luck.

"I'll give him my favorite toy ladybug. Quack, Chuck, quack!" But she had no luck.

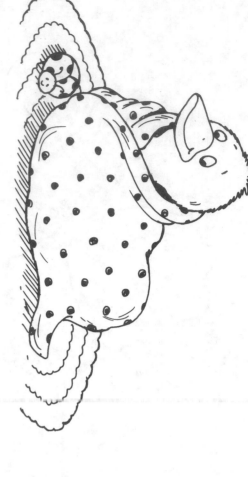

"I'll set him on a cozy rug. Quack, Chuck, quack!" But she had no luck.

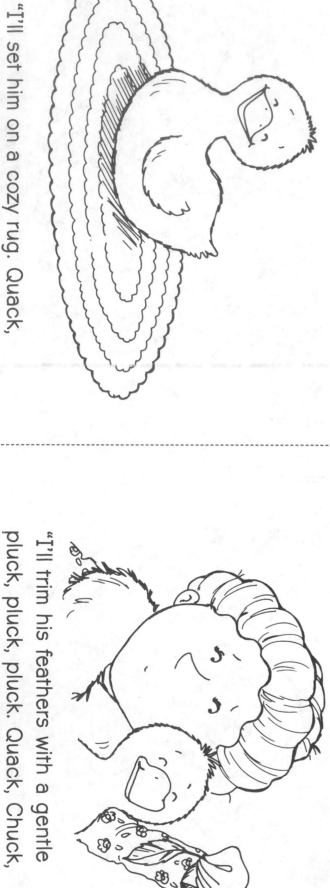

"I'll tuck him into bed. Quack, Chuck, quack!" But she had no luck.

"I'll trim his feathers with a gentle pluck, pluck, pluck. Quack, Chuck, quack!" But she had no luck.